BELIEVE IN YOURSELF!

R.SAISRINIDHI

Made with ♥ on the Notion Press Platform
www.notionpress.com

Introduction

"To be yourself in a world that is constantly trying to make you something else is the greatest accomplishment" - UNKNOWN

"Think before you do something or else you will regret it later" – R.Saisrinidhi.

R.Saisrinidhi is studying in 8th grade, a youngest Novelist and Motivational speaker, based in India, Chennai.

Contents

CHAPTER I

Life is so Precious

Life is so Precious!
This story was based on real incidents,
Let's see what happened.
One day a girl was born to Mrs.Alina and Mr.Shark and they named her Shaanvi. Her grandparents lived together. Shaanvi was not mature when reached 6th grade. When she was promoted to 7th grade in June 2021, she thought that she wants to become a singer. She started talking to mirror herself like "she loves herself", "she motivated herself", and she encouraged herself in tough situations.

In January 2022, she became mature and realized some of her fake friends. She had many haters but she told herself "I don't care what others think of me". She made it clear and loved herself a lot.

One day she went to Lord Ganesha's temple and prayed to become a singer and wished to help poor people. She worked hard and studied more for that and finally she became a singer and helped poor people. Later, on stage, she told that "Believe in yourself".

The moral of the story: "Don't Care what others say, just do what makes you happy"

Chapter - 2

A village girl wants to become a tennis player will she be able to do it?

Let's see in this story

She is from the united kingdom, Genteigh village. Her name is Amelia she was studying 10th she have no interest in studies she was an orphan she was in the orphanage, her mother and father died when she was a year, her aunt is an orphanage officer but her aunt always being rude to her. she begs her aunt to join tennis academy she told ok finally.

Amelia was so happy after that she was practicing very hard but she failed that time she remembered Mr.Michel –B JordanNo: 1 Baseket ball player he failed she missed more than 9000 shots in her career. He lost almost 300 games and 26 times but he succeed and got 5 awards as an American player, So Amelia got motivation from him. she is now 11 th grade, and she really got tired of being a failure all scolded her but her face was like a strong girl and got 100 failures.

She herself said the only one is 'I don't care what others think I will do what makes me happy, so she just focus on winning a no .1 tennis player, she worked so hard finally went to the district level and got 1st prize and she, went to the state level, after 5 yrs of tennis she went to international level and got 1st prize. Then all media just asked her who is your inspiration she told Michael B Jordan they told hmm.. okay.

where are you from she told from UK cranliegh village and I don't have my mom and dad they died at that time *her aunt saw a she really turned kind after seeing her stepdaughter Amelia just told one thing to the media and all I was failed but I didn't cure I motivated myself I love myself Really none supported me, I just supported myself, "Be yourself".*

Chapter 3

Do the best you can

When you got a dream you have got to grab it and achieve it. You will be unstoppable when you start believing in yourself. If you can dream it you can do it just believe in yourself. when no one believes you start to believe in yourself that's what makes you a winner .actually 2 yrs to 3 years back who is negative and didn't hear about any positive kinds of stuff but later one day I heard it gave positive stuff but later one day. I heard it gave me positive life. I learned that negative life can gives you a positive life. I experienced it most so, before taking a decision think about it because you should not regret that in the future. I adore this quote

"Do what you can, with what you have, where you are" Theodore Roosevelt

I can tell you that one day you can hear or read a story on Spotify about motivation and then see the change in yourself. I am pretty sure it will work "Kill them with your success bury them with your smile"

Trust yourself that you can do it & get it –BAZ Luhrmann.

"If you are doing the right thing then you should not care what others think of you"

You can ask me what if we care about others think of just remember.

Then I am sure you can't live your life happily.

- *When you are alone, mind your thoughts*
- *When you are with your friends, mind your tongue*

- *When you are angry, mind your temper.*
- *When you are with a group, mind your behavior*
- *When you are in trouble, mind your emotions*
- *When god starts blessings you, mind your ego.*

Just stop comparing yourself with others, just say I am the best version of myself and the most vital part is I love myself more than anyone.

Be confident.

Chapter 4

Once was a beginner!

Hello Everyone! This is aria and gonna tell my story let's begin! I will tell you about me first I love to write, I love to sing, and I have many bobbies too, I have a family we are all living in Germany, My ambition is to become a singer and (Start a business) and my passion be a motivational speaker and to traveling the world. Let's start my family. My mom's name is luna my father's name is Ryan, we are a family living in Germany. Mostly some people will talk well in front of me but when I went they will talk badly 'don't trust this kind of person. At first, I am a little shy, but later I am a confident girl and motivator how have I become like this it is a simple example to tell how to find out if a person is talking behind your back. It's simple they will gossip about another person to you, so in that self, you should find that person can talk behind your back at any time. Maybe they can.

I have had this experience in my life, do you know anything, about many achievers who have to achieve their goals and desires? They all have only one mantra which is "Never give up" one day everything will come to change whenever life gives tough situations face it you can...Being yourself is good. I love to write but many people rejected me I learned something maybe you can fall 6 times but get up in 8 eight. Whatever happened never give up and never lose hope I learned. I am the inspiration for myself in my life my mom used to tell me that in teenage until you become 18yrs old infacuation so, I replied to her that god will send me someone who deserves she smiled! Let's come to this topic. I told to myself that every day is a new beginning take a deep breath smile start again. So everyone rejected me but 1 phone call changed my entire life. I was so glad at that moment. I told to myself" everything happens for a reason" That positive vibes changed my life I am a author now.

Moral: Whatever happened that is good or bad take it easy and move on." One small positive thought can change your whole day" Be kind to all.

"No worries " HAKUNA MATATA

Chapter 5

Believe in yourself Startup (PART 1)

I am going to tell you all about my own story let's go actually I am having a dream to become a singer and to start a business and travel this world anyways, really this is a story of mine and what I learned from it let me tell you. In my flat, no one likes me they are all jealous when seeing me in that personal experience. I got to know what his friends are and who are fake and true. Now let me give you come to explain how to find true or fake friends. Fake friends always talk behind your back or they will tell your secrets to everyone and do gossiping. you can ask me how to find your friend who is talking behind your back. Here it is experienced in my real life will tell you now., if someone talks bad about their friends and is with you at that time you should be alert, be careful with them. In my flat, they judged me and talked badly about me behind my back so you can ask why you didn't get angry nope. I didn't know why? Because of this mantra

DON'T CARE WHAT OTHERS THINK OF YOU IS NONE OF YOUR BUSINESS. I will always tell myself that when I am angry close my eyes every day is a new beginning start again and smile. I learned in my life to accept reality and move on you know what I am a short temper now also but not like me in the past. Really want to tell you that 'don't judge a book by its Cover.

IF YOU CAN DREAM IT, YOU CAN DO IT.

Now also I am thinking like god I want to become a singer and start a business and travel the world. I have a doubt that how can small girl can achieve a big goal and that time I remembered this quote. WHEN NO ONE BELIEVE IN YOU, JUST START TO BELIEVE IN YOURSELF.that's what makes you the winner. My mom will always tell motivational speakers but I am not sure about the quotes I am using when I wake up in the morning at 5 AM.

? IAM THE BEST
? I am the winner
? Today is my day
? God is always with me
? I can,I will
? Love yourself

Chapter 6

The beginner (Part 2)

When life gives you tough you just stay (Don't care) whatever can happen no one can dare to stop me just say out of my no matter what I am going to achieve what I want just to get out always in life all cant life you in life some can like and some cant just be you, Do you, For you

From the age of 13 to 18, whatever you are going through is temporary all you need is to love yourself no matter what. If you believe in yourself then you are unstoppable no one stop you from your dream only you'

"This quote I admire from APJ ABDUL Kalam"

? Confidence may not bring you success but it can make you face every problem.

The way you see yourself matters

Remember this no matter who you or where you are just speak yourself

(VIBE aLONE UNTIL YOU HAVE VALUED) RM

This all makes me more powerful and even more confidence"Never stop dreaming" Dream big.

Love the life you live in present – R.Saisrinidhi

There is no real excellence in all this world which can be seprated from right thing. Time heals everything buddy

Life is small you don't know when you will die so, live the life the way you want.

This is your life just decide you want be happy or not anyways happiness is just a choice whether you choose it or not.

Be happy the way you are

Chapter 7

This is about a real incident, lets go of the story,

? Surrounded yourself with positive people because when you surround yourself with them you will also get positive energy. So I am going to tell a quote about this.

A mirror reflects a man's face, but what he is really like is shown by the kind of friends he chooses

So, here an instance of this when a boy is in school he to be want to become a scientist his friends laugh at him and told you can't achieve anything, totally you are a loser! This is a clear example you can only a person can decide where should your environment belongs.

Things around you helping you towards success or are they holding you back? – W. Clement stone.

When you are with negative people ask yourself why am I choose to be with them. By the way, I think it's good to help someone overcome their negativity. But if you have been trying for several years and aren't getting anywhere. And it's time to move on.

Succcess is going from failure to failure without loss of enthusiasm – Winston Churchill.

Success is a series of small coins.

Always remember success won't come after you wake up in the morning success won't come overnight, It takes time all you want is patience to wait great things take time so, never gives up! If you have a lot of money you just keep buying cars that are not a real success. Real success is you have money and helping others that are the only stuff that defines who you are.

You can get everything in life you want if you'll just help enough other people get what they want – Zig Ziglar

CHAPTER VIII

Chapter 8

Introduction:

Do you always remember wondering why life is hard? In my personal experience, I asked life and it smiled back and told me that only happiness is not life but sadness is also part of life. I mean, good is a part of life like bad is also part of life. For instance, Amelia went to the coffee shop she sat and ordered coffee but the coffee came late waiter asked for sorry to Amelia, and Amelia smiled and told to the waiter it was okay no problem! On the same day David also came to the coffee shop sat and ordered but the waiter came late, David scolded and gave a bad rating about the coffee shop. Notice the difference no matter how you see the world. The world will return back, understood it! Okay, let's get started.

Come to the story, Actually, I always thought about a small middle-class girl and how she is going to achieve her desire okay anyways, that girl's name is ava Gabriella she has a goal of becoming a singer and starting a business and want to travel this world she has three desire's she have been graduated now and she went to an interview and there all rejected her she tried all but last rejected, she has a habit of reading the book that time she found a quote here it is be happy the way you are, "A positive attitude is a personal passport to a better tomorrow. Rejection is the first step of success. – Unknown".

She read this quote and god motivated that's my spirit her heart told so this is what we should learn at last what will happen you win. How? if you stay positive in a negative situation you win, she won after a lot of bad circumstances from here we should. I hope you can understand this! Do you know that quote words are, of course, the most powerful drug used by mankind – RUDYARD KIPLING

Here is one more quote" Success seems to be largely a matter of hanging on after others have let go – William feather.

Ara finally she woned, she become a singer and started a business and travel, she has done it. Failure is not the opposite of success it's part of success.

She told this world the stage she told many people humiliated me because of my past stuff but I didn't give up I tried my best in everything finally I came up here and I am seeing thousands of people yet, my dream came true. I always dream of coming to this stage and want to give a speech about my journey buddy I gave now. So whatever happens "ACCEPT THE REALITY, and MOVE ON" is what I learned from my childhood.

Never give up.

Chapter 9

Failure

I realized that some are temporary and some are permanent always mind it. whenever you are saying sorry to someone remember that you should repeat the same mistake in your life. Whatever you are going through now is not permanent see, it problem that came into your life god gave you 2 choices 1 solving it 2nd is overthinking it and not doing your work properly always just keep a desire then turn not doing your work properly always just keep a desire then turn it to the aim. One day you will be unstoppable you will definitely achieve what you want to be. If you are not kind to yourself then you can't really be kind to others one day I asked god that gives me some good lessons he showed it today how to behave and at that moment I realized I can achieve my goal in front of the person who dislikes me I want to grow stronger no one can stop me from my dreams god is always with me I will definitely make my dream come true and this confidence gives me goosebumps do you know that I had a dream to get an award in my school one day I have been participating music competition in my school and the unexpected moment came up and they told me that I won the 2nd prize that proud moment and after 3 days I went to stage and principal told congrats dear that moment I can't express my feelings but anyways in this I got a small lesson if you can dream it you can do it failures makes a successful person. life is very short enjoy a bit of it. being is a choice.

The moral of the lesson is" I can I will this my day god is always with me I am the best in the winner.

This is the motivation mantra I will tell this whenever I wake up in the morning.

Chapter 10

Struggle in life

Do you feel stressed out and in a depression okay now I am going to tell you about my personal incident 2 years before o was in a severe depression about no one liking me. So after some months people
(I just don't want to mention the names) started talking bad about me in the back, and they self left me and the friendship. This made me realize who is true and fake. 1 yr before I was comparing myself with someone else but now I am telling myself I am the best version of myself notice this how I become like this 2 years I have a negative attitude before 1 year I have positive and negative but now I have only positive attitude so let me give you some examples to explain the difference between positive and negative attitude.

- *The person with the negative attitude thinks "I cant*
- *The person with the positive attitude thinks I can*
- *The person with a negative attitude dwells on problems*
- *A person with a positive attitude concentrates on solutions*

You cant always control circumstances. But you can control your own thoughts.

A happy person is not a person in a certain set of circumstances but rather a person with a certain set of attitudes.

Let's get started

How you are treating [people;e. No matter how educated you are or talented rich or cool you believe you are how you treat people ultimately tells about you. Integrity is everything. Success begins in the mind the power of attitude can change your destiny so now visualize in yourself what you should achieve just close your eyes and make a desire what you want in your life., the most pleasant quote I used often in my life. Be happy the way you are

Laugh often and smile big.

This happened to me a month before had a good experience.

If you can dream it you can do it I hope you like this.